Examining Mass Shootings

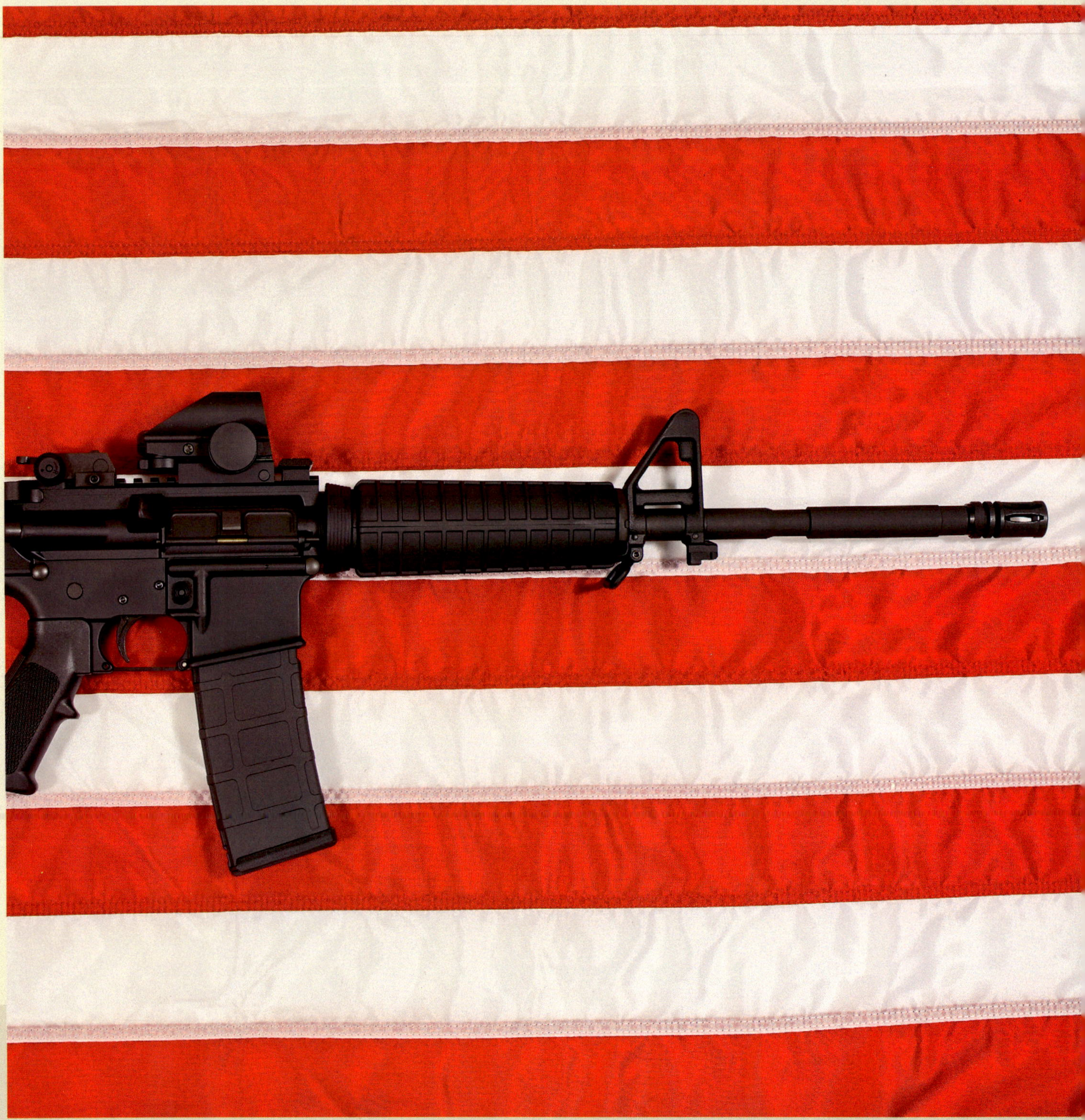

Examining Mass Shootings

Lisa M. Bolt Simons

Living in AMERICA

CREATIVE EDUCATION
CREATIVE PAPERBACKS

Published by Creative Education and Creative Paperbacks
P.O. Box 227, Mankato, Minnesota 56002
Creative Education and Creative Paperbacks are imprints
of The Creative Company
www.thecreativecompany.us

Book design by Graham Morgan (www.bluedes.com)
Art direction by Tom Morgan
Edited by Jill Kalz

Images by AP Newsroom (Evan Frost/Minnesota Public Radio), Getty (AAron Ontiveroz/The Denver Post, Arturo Jimenez/Anadolu Agency, Drew Angerer, Jahi Chikwendiu/The Washington Post, Michael Ciaglo, Nathan Posner/Anadolu Agency, Win McNamee), THE INSTITUTE FOR HEALTH METRICS AND EVALUATION (IHME) (Scott Glenn), Pexels (Bob Price, cottonbro studio, Emma Guliani, Karolina Grabowska), Shutterstock (ja-images), Statista, Unsplash (Chip Vincent, David von Diemar, Jay Rembert), Wikimedia Commons (James Tourtellotte/U.S. Customs and Border Protection, pml2008, San Bernardino County Sheriff's Department, Tom Lankes)

Copyright © 2025 Creative Education, Creative Paperbacks
International copyright reserved in all countries.
No part of this book may be reproduced in any form
without written permission from the publisher.

Library of Congress Cataloging-in-Publication Data
Names: Simons, Lisa M. Bolt, 1969– author.
Title: Examining mass shootings / Lisa M. Bolt Simons.
Description: Mankato, Minnesota : Creative Education and Creative Paperbacks, [2025] | Series: Living in America | Includes bibliographical references and index. | Audience: Ages 12–15 | Audience: Grades 7–9 | Summary: "A social studies title for young adults that examines the history of mass shootings in the United States, mass murder motives, and America's gun control debate. Includes sidebars, real-person profiles, a glossary, a timeline, and further resources"—Provided by publisher.
Identifiers: LCCN 2023047115 (print) | LCCN 2023047116 (ebook) | ISBN 9781640269071 (library binding) | ISBN 9781682774571 (paperback) | ISBN 9798889890751 (ebook)
Subjects: LCSH: Mass shootings—United States—Juvenile literature. | Violent crimes—United States—Juvenile literature. | Firearms—Law and legislation—United States—Juvenile literature. | Gun control—United States—Juvenile literature.
Classification: LCC HV7436 .S566 2025 (print) | LCC HV7436 (ebook) | DDC 364.152/340973—dc23/eng/20231102
LC record available at https://lccn.loc.gov/2023047115
LC ebook record available at https://lccn.loc.gov/2023047116

Printed in China

STANDING ON THE SIDE OF
LOVE
THROW
AWAY YOUR
#ENOUGH
LOVE YOUR
KIDS NOT
YOUR GUNS
ENOUGH

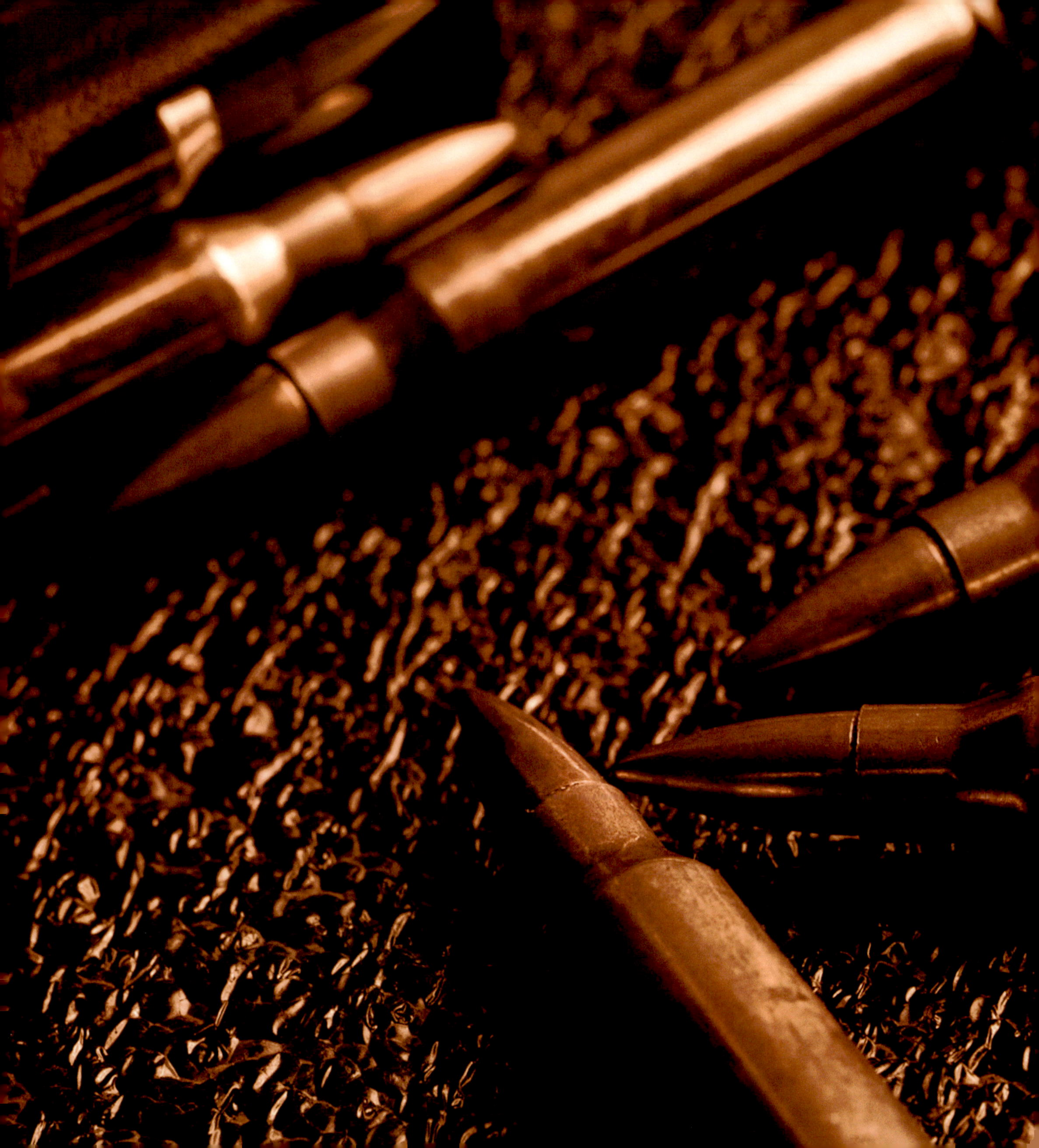

CONTENTS

Introduction	8
Chapter 1: A Deadly, Shrinking Timeline	11
ZOOM IN: MASS SHOOTINGS THROUGH THE YEARS	14
ZOOM IN: LAS VEGAS, 2017	18
Chapter 2: Schools Beyond Columbine	21
ZOOM IN: ACTIVE SHOOTER DRILLS	24
ZOOM IN: VIOLENCE AT HOME	28
Chapter 3: The Root Cause	31
ZOOM IN: DEFINE "MILITIA"	34
ZOOM IN: UNITED STATES FIRST IN GUN DEATHS	38
Chapter 4: Finding Solutions	40
ZOOM IN: NO NAMES	42
Getting Real:	44
SUE KLEBOLD	44
DR. JILLIAN PETERSON AND DR. JAMES DENSLEY	45
Timeline	46
Glossary	47
Selected Bibliography	47
Websites	47
Index	48

Introduction

It was the morning of September 6, 1949. Military veteran Howard Unruh took a 9mm pistol, left the apartment he shared with his mom in Camden, New Jersey, and murdered 13 people as he walked down the street. He was 28 years old. His younger brother later told reporters that after Unruh returned from serving his country, he hadn't been the same.

As defined by the Federal Bureau of Investigations (FBI), a mass murder is when four or more people are killed during a single incident. A mass shooting is when four or more people are wounded or killed, not including the shooter. Between 1966 and 2012, almost one-third of the world's mass shooters were from the United States, but the country itself has only 5 percent of the world population.

The topic of mass shootings is a divisive one. Mass shootings represent only a small number of gun incidents, but they headline the news because of the number of people wounded and killed at one time. People disagree about how best to stop gun violence. There are those who believe in restricting who can buy a gun and what kind. There are others who believe in the right to bear arms. Researchers, lawmakers, concerned citizens, and grieving families are trying to figure out how to compromise on policies that will prevent future mass shootings.

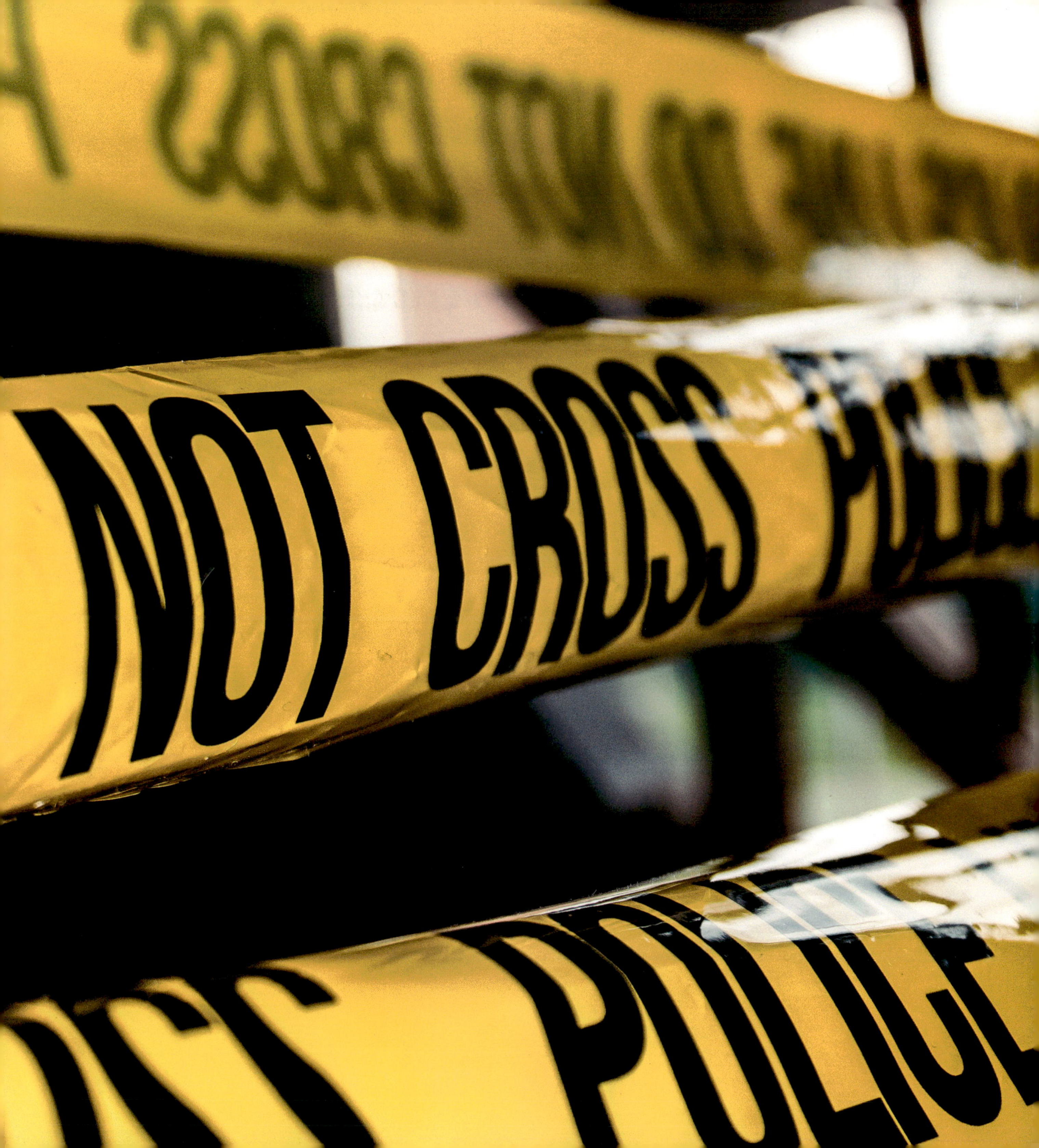
NOT CROSS

A woman tries to hide during the 1966 University of Texas at Austin shooting.

CHAPTER 1:

A Deadly, Shrinking Timeline

Years ago, the time between mass shootings in the United States was nearly two decades. After the 1949 shooting **rampage** in New Jersey, the country didn't see another one for 17 years.

On August 1, 1966, another 20-something veteran stabbed his mother to death and then his wife. He then climbed the clock tower on the campus of the University of Texas at Austin, where he was a student, and shot three people there. Next, he shot and killed 14 people on the observation deck. He also wounded more than 30 people.

Eighteen years later, the first "modern" mass shooting happened.

On July 18, 1984, a 41-year-old man living in California told his wife he was going to go "hunting humans." He drove to a San Ysidro McDonald's restaurant and starting shooting people with a shotgun, a semiautomatic pistol, and a variation of an Uzi submachine gun. Police responded right away, but they were unable to enter the restaurant. They were also unable to subdue the shooter. A sniper did kill him 77 minutes later, but by the time the bloodshed was over, 19 people had been wounded and 21 people killed. Five of those 21 murder victims were children under the age of 11, including an 8-month-old baby.

After the McDonald's incident, the time between mass shootings in the United States started shrinking. It was only seven years later when the next tragedy struck.

On October 16, 1991, a man drove his pickup truck through the window of a busy Luby's restaurant in Killeen, Texas. He then jumped out of his truck and started shooting customers. Targeting mostly women, he wounded 20 people and killed 23. The man was later described by people who knew him as **paranoid** and filled with hatred for women.

Eight years passed before one of the most infamous mass shootings in U.S. history occurred. The place was Columbine High School in Littleton, Colorado. On April 20, 1999, two teenagers entered the school through the cafeteria. They shot fellow students and teachers using shotguns and semiautomatic weapons. They ended up in the library, where many students had fled. There they killed 13 individuals before taking their own lives. More than 30 mass shooters over the next 20 years would cite the two Columbine teenagers as inspiration for their own crimes.

Another school shooting happened at Virginia Tech on April 16, 2007. A student first killed two people in a dormitory room. Campus police didn't notify the student body about it because the

Protesters outside the Colorado State Capitol urge lawmakers to ban assault weapons and stop gun violence in schools.

12 — EXAMINING MASS SHOOTINGS

GRADUATIONS, NOT FUNERALS!
COLORADO EDUCATION ASSOCIATION
DCTA
SCHOOLS ARE FOR LEARNING NOT LOCK-DOWNS
HOW LOUD DO THE [illegible] HAVE TO BE BEFORE YOU [illegible]
TEACHERS AND FAMILIES
ND GUN
ENCE NOW!

ZOOM IN: MASS SHOOTINGS THROUGH THE YEARS

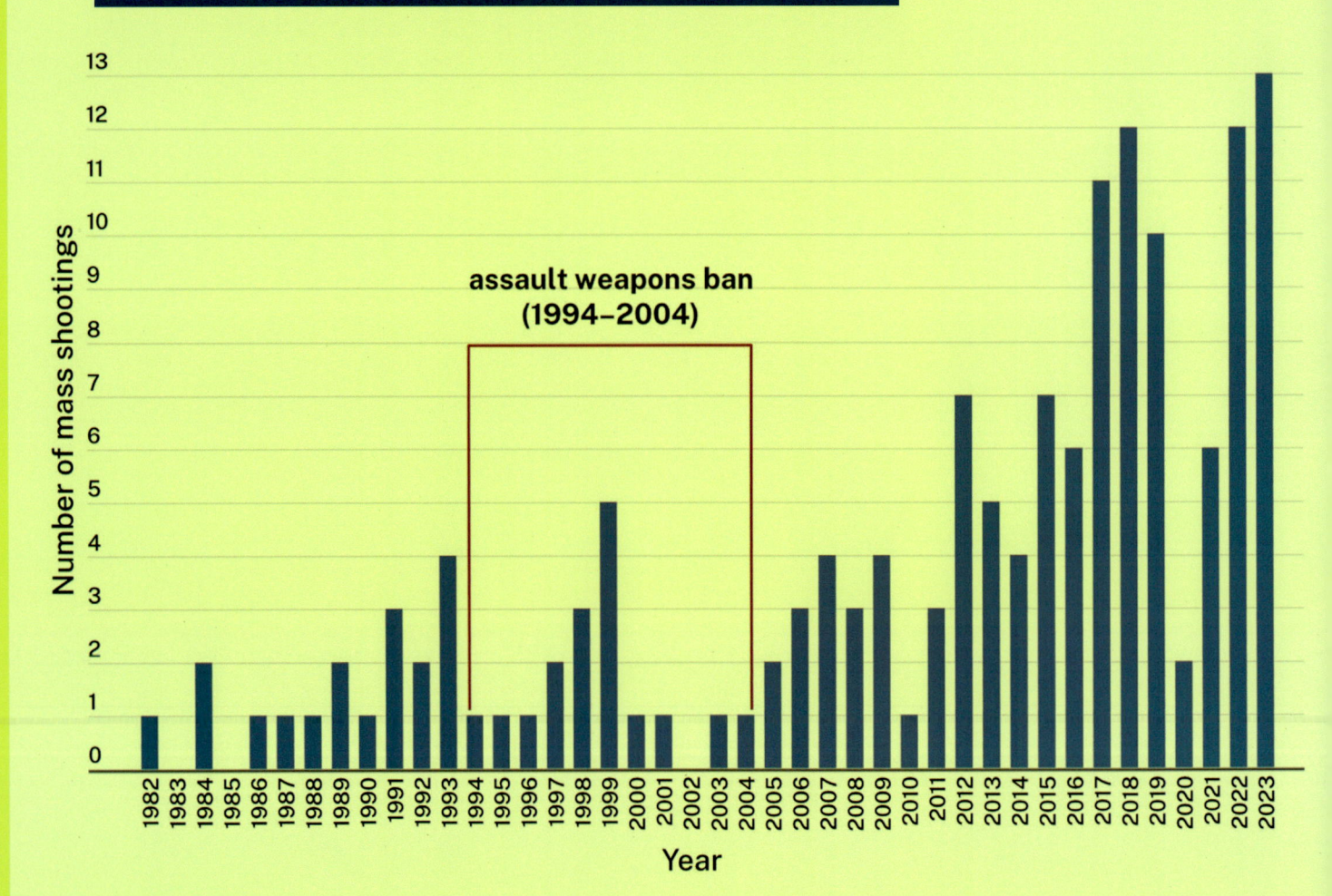

assault weapons ban (1994–2004)

shooting seemed like an isolated event. Unbeknownst to them, however, something else was happening. For two and half hours, the shooter gathered more ammunition and mailed a manifesto to NBC News in New York City. He then walked into an engineering building and barricaded himself in a classroom. With a pair of semiautomatic pistols, he wounded 17 people and killed 30 before taking his own life.

Not three years later, on November 5, 2009, a shooter walked into a medical center at Fort Hood, Texas. He was a 39-year-old psychiatrist in the U.S. Army who had become an extremist. He started shooting a handgun he had fitted with two laser sights, injuring 32 people and killing 13, including a woman who was pregnant. The shooter was shot and paralyzed by a civilian police officer.

Terror then shattered the sense of security at a movie theater on July 20, 2012. At a midnight screening in Aurora, Colorado, a 24-year-old man dressed in body armor walked in through an exit door with three guns. He wounded more than 70 moviegoers and killed 12. He had also rigged his apartment with explosives. He pleaded insanity and avoided the death penalty for his crimes.

A racially motivated act struck a house of worship almost three years later. On June 17, 2015, a Bible study group welcomed a 21-year-old white man into the Emanuel African Methodist Episcopal Church in Charleston, South Carolina. The man sat quietly for about 15 minutes before taking out his pistol, firing 70 rounds, and killing 9 Black worshippers. Victims included the church's senior

Mass shootings slowed during a 10-year assault weapons ban, suggesting that restrictions do help protect people.

pastor and a state senator. The shooter ran out of the church and drove off. He was captured the next morning, 245 miles (394 kilometers) north of Charleston—a Confederate flag and a burned U.S. flag in his car. During a taped confession, he laughed several times about what he had done.

Months later, in California, a 2015 company Christmas party at the Inland Regional Center in San Bernardino turned deadly. With semiautomatic weapons and two pistols, a married couple wounded 21 co-workers and killed 14. They fled the scene and were later killed in a shootout with police. It is believed the husband, an American, and his wife, a Pakistani, had converted to extremist beliefs several years before. Their family members and friends expressed shock at the horrific crime, especially, they said, since the couple had welcomed a baby just six months before.

The first mass shooting to target the **LGBTQ+** community happened in Orlando, Florida, in 2016. The shooter had previously been investigated by the FBI. He had been put on a watch list for possibly being a terrorist, but no evidence had been found. He was able to buy weapons. He entered the Pulse nightclub on June 12 with a semiautomatic rifle and a semiautomatic handgun. The shooter wounded more than 50

Handguns and semiautomatic rifles used during the 2015 San Bernardino, California, shooting

people and killed 49. He was finally killed after a three-hour standoff with police. He left behind a three-year-old son.

On November 5, 2017, horror struck the First Baptist Church in Sutherland Springs, Texas. Armed with an AR-style semiautomatic rifle, a shooter wounded 20 people and killed 26 in just 11 minutes. On October 27, 2018, the Tree of Life Synagogue in Pittsburgh, Pennsylvania, saw 2 worshippers wounded and 11 killed in a racially motivated attack.

Ten months later, on August 3, 2019, a man drove 11 hours from the Dallas, Texas, area to a Walmart in El Paso. Before he entered the store, armed with an AK-47, he posted a racist manifesto on a social media site that allowed hate speech. It was clear he had purposely targeted El Paso's large Latino community. He wounded 22 people and killed 23.

A DEADLY, SHRINKING TIMELINE — 17

ZOOM IN: LAS VEGAS, 2017

The United States didn't see its worst mass shooting until October 1, 2017, in Las Vegas, Nevada. That night, 22,000 country music fans sang and danced to live music. One man, who was a retired postal service worker, accountant, real estate investor, and high-stakes gambler, fired more than 1,000 rounds into the crowd from the 32nd floor of a hotel suite across the street. In 11 minutes, the 64-year-old shooter wounded more than 400 people (another 450 were hurt escaping the terror) and killed 58. As the police closed in on his hotel suite, the shooter killed himself. He left no note or clue about the motive for his crime.

Grocery stores were the scene of mass shootings in Boulder, Colorado, in 2021 and Buffalo, New York, in 2022. In Colorado, a man wounded 26 and killed 10, including the first police officer who arrived at the scene. The shooter was later diagnosed with schizophrenia and treated in a state mental hospital. The shooter in New York, only 18 years old, **livestreamed** his attack on his social media account. He wounded 3 shoppers, and all 10 people killed were Black.

Eight months later, on January 21, 2023, people celebrating Lunar New Year's Eve in Monterey Park, California, were terrorized. A 72-year-old shooter opened fire in a dance studio, wounding 10 people and killing 10. He then drove to another dance studio where people were celebrating and tried to shoot again, but community members there wrestled away his gun. The man fled the scene in a van. By the time officers caught up to him, the shooter had shot and killed himself.

The many incidents mentioned in this chapter represent only a fraction of the mass shootings that have happened in the United States to date. *Mother Jones* magazine maintains a list of mass killings that have happened since 1982. As of December 2023, the list included 149 mass shootings.

Site of the 2017 Las Vegas, Nevada, mass shooting

MANDALAY BAY
MANDALAY BAY
DELANO
MANDALAY BAY
LUXOR
MJ LIVE
NEXT FROM
NASHVILLE

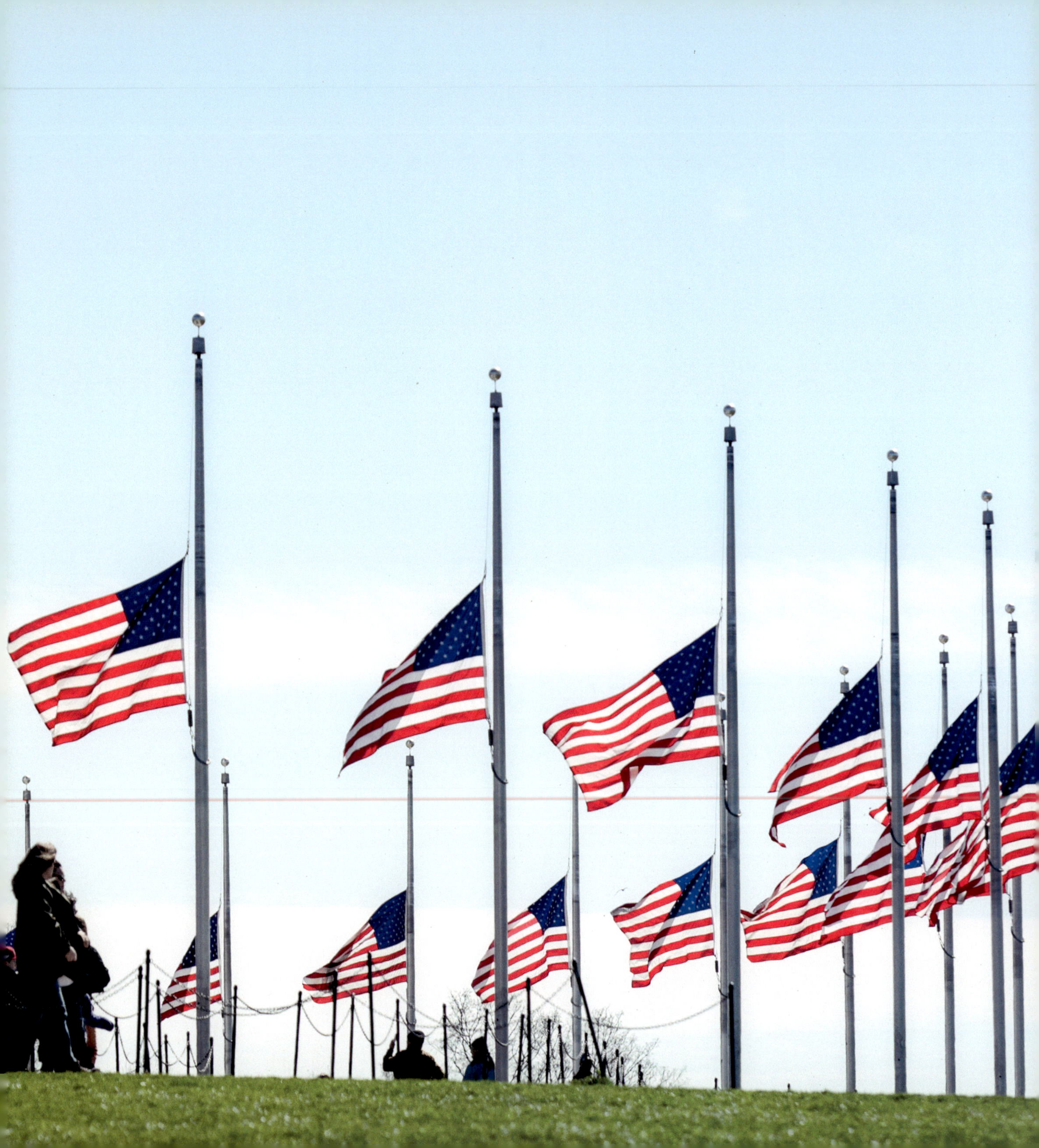

CHAPTER 2:

Schools Beyond Columbine

The mass shooting that unfolded at Columbine High School on April 20, 1999, was planned in detail for a year.

The shooters had supposedly been bullied, including being on the receiving end of objects thrown from moving cars. They videotaped themselves describing what they'd do to get back at these bullies, but they also apologized in advance to their parents.

Besides having explosives on their bodies, both young men carried "cricket" and other types of bombs into the school. The small cricket bombs caused bits of metal, called shrapnel, to hit and injure people. Bigger propane and pipe bombs were intended to cause explosions that would kill many more victims. Police later defused 30 of these bombs in the school and in cars in the parking lot. During the 45 minutes of terror at Columbine, the two student shooters fired more than 900 rounds.

U.S. flags fly at half-staff to honor the victims of mass shootings.

The Columbine incident came at a time before the social media we know today existed. The news was largely televised live around the United States, shocking the nation. But it wasn't the first school shooting in U.S. history.

The earliest known school shooting happened on July 26, 1764. Four American Indians shot and killed a **schoolmaster** and several children inside a Pennsylvania schoolhouse. The morning of November 2, 1853, in Louisville, Kentucky, a student bought a self-cocking pistol. He took it to school and killed his schoolmaster because the teacher had punished the shooter's brother the day before. On July 4, 1884, a student shot and killed a fellow student at Sunday school in Charleston, South Carolina, for talking badly about her.

There were a number of instances in the 1800s of students shooting their teachers to avoid being punished. The first known *mass* shooting in a school happened on April 9, 1891. A 70-year-old man fired a shotgun at children playing at recess in Newburgh, New York. Several children were injured. Most school attacks during the 1800s, however, involved the attackers hitting the victims with stones or stabbing them with knives. In the early 1900s, attackers often used fire or explosives.

In the 1970s, two school mass shootings involved the police. The first few days of May 1970, Kent State students were protesting the Vietnam War (1955–75) and the U.S. invasion of Cambodia. Because of violent **confrontations** between the police and students, the governor of Ohio sent the National Guard to the college campus in Columbus. On May 4, thousands of students gathered to protest both the war and the presence of the National Guard. When the demonstrators were told to leave, they threw rocks. Tear gas was thrown at the students. The guardsmen seemed to leave but then turned and started firing their weapons. Nine Kent State students were injured, and four were killed.

A father carries a picture of his son, who was killed in the 2012 Sandy Hook school shooting, past the empty chairs of other victims.

JOSE FLORES JR
4TH GRADE
MR REYES
MRS MIRELES
4TH GRADE
ROOM 112

Ten days later, Black college students in Mississippi were allegedly throwing rocks at white drivers. Police went to Jackson State University, a predominantly Black campus, to investigate. Students and non-students alike threw rocks and bricks. Police fired more than 400 rounds. Twelve people were injured. A high school senior and a junior at the college were killed.

Only a few school shootings with multiple victims occurred during the early 1980s. However, things shifted in the 1990s. Incidents grew worse. During the 1998–99 school year, 3,523 students were expelled for bringing a gun to school. Of those, 57 percent were in high school, 33 percent in middle school, and 10 percent in elementary school. Gun violence at schools increased into the early 1990s.

Most school shooters acted alone. But on March 24, 1998, two boys, ages 11 and 13, pulled the fire alarm at their school in Jonesboro, Arkansas. As their classmates and teachers left the building, the two boys hid in the woods and shot at them. Ten people were wounded. Four students and one teacher died.

Even though schools around the country had implemented "active shooter drills" since the Columbine mass shooting,

> **ZOOM IN: ACTIVE SHOOTER DRILLS**
>
> Active shooter drills have become commonplace in today's schools. Students, teachers, and staff practice them each school year. Usually, a shooter drill includes locking doors, shutting off lights, and sheltering in place. Some schools have students barricade the doors and grab objects such as pencils or scissors to defend themselves. Drills may include fake gunshots or blood, although these additions have been increasingly criticized as being more harmful to students' mental health than helpful. In 2023, Minnesota passed a law that allowed students to opt out of shooter drills. New Jersey and Washington had taken similar steps.

Members of law enforcement use an empty school to practice what to do during an active shooter situation.

nothing could prepare people for the shock of what happened on December 14, 2012. On that day, Sandy Hook Elementary, in Newtown, Connecticut, was forever linked to gun violence.

The 20-year-old shooter, who lived with his mother near Sandy Hook, had struggled for years with multiple **psychiatric** issues. The morning of December 14, he murdered his mother while she slept, stole several of her guns, and drove her car to the elementary school. Then he shot his way through a window next to the locked front door to enter the building. After killing the principal and the school psychologist, the shooter went into a classroom and killed a teacher and 14 students. He entered a second classroom,

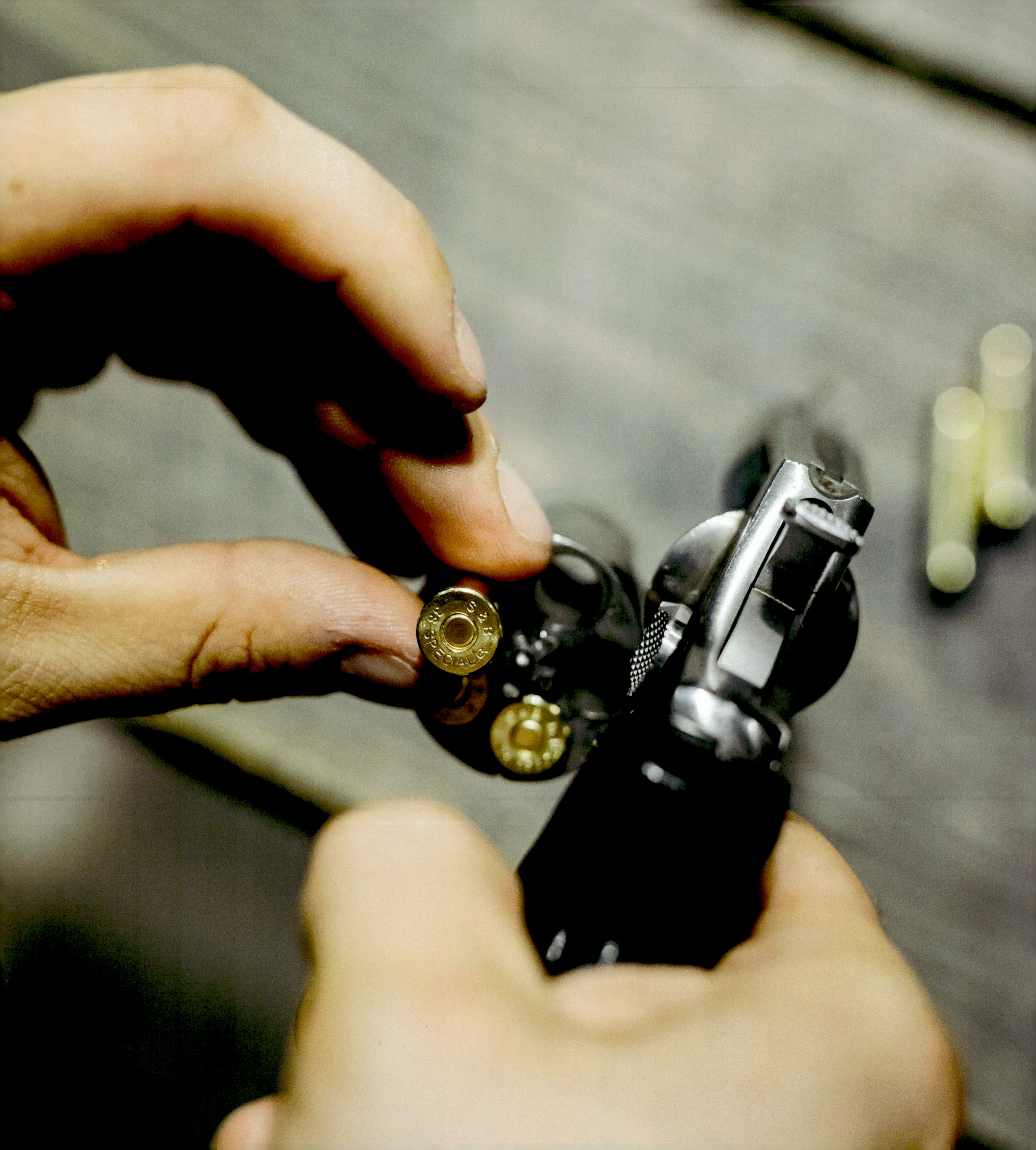

killing three adults and six children who tried to run. He fired 154 rounds, mostly with an AR-15, in less than 5 minutes before killing himself with a handgun.

Six years later, on Valentine's Day 2018, a 19-year-old started shooting an AR-15 outside Marjory Stoneman Douglas High School in Parkland, Florida. He then entered the school, injuring 14 people and killing 17. As students fled the scene, he blended in with them but was captured an hour later. He had recently been expelled from the school.

More school horror happened four years later. On May 24, 2022, an 18-year-old shooter walked in a back door at Robb Elementary in Uvalde, Texas, carrying an AR-15. He opened fire, wounding 17 people and killing 2 teachers and 19 children. He was killed by police.

Although safety **protocols** and procedures have changed since Columbine, schools are still trying to figure out how to best handle shooter situations. It's an ongoing process. Most schools today have school resource officers. These armed guards work with the student body to prevent shootings from happening in the first place. Also, new protocols instruct local law enforcement teams to enter schools immediately to stop shooters as quickly as possible. In the past, news of an active shooter often caused chaos, with a flood of 911 calls, responders communicating on different radio channels, and police officers waiting outside for SWAT teams to arrive. Because of that chaos, the two Columbine shooters had 47 minutes to freely carry out their crimes; the Robb Elementary shooter had 75 minutes—*after* police arrived.

Some school districts are taking protection a step further, by arming staff members. This controversial policy does not necessarily

Training staff members to use a firearm may or may not be a good way to protect students from active shooters.

> ### ZOOM IN: VIOLENCE AT HOME
>
> People may think that mass shootings are random. But too often, the violence stems from domestic issues. Studies have found that in 46 percent of mass shootings involving four or more victims, the killer shot a former partner or family member. Just over 68 percent of mass shootings are domestic violence issues or the killer has a history of domestic violence. Moreover, there tend to be more deaths at the scene of a mass shooting when domestic violence is at the core of the attack.

mean that an educator is carrying a firearm. Only those staff members who have volunteered and gone through extensive training can access strategically placed firearms in an emergency. Gun owners often support this method of protection. However, researchers at Hamline University in St. Paul, Minnesota, found that "the rate of deaths was 2.83 times greater in schools with an armed guard present." Further, "[A]n armed officer on the scene was the number one factor associated with increased casualties after the [shooters'] use of assault rifles or submachine guns." The researchers also believe the shooters are most likely suicidal and see armed officers or personnel as a challenge, not an obstacle.

Because of the increasing number of mass shootings, school life has changed in many ways, including the addition of active shooter drills, metal detectors, and bulletproof backpacks. Daily life has changed, too. Bag restrictions and checks at sporting events and concerts is the new normal. Security has increased in courthouses and other state and federal buildings. People at shopping malls, movie theaters, and entertainment venues of all sizes instinctively look for exits and escape routes, just in case of emergency.

Because of their unpredictability, domestic violence calls are some of the most dangerous calls for police officers to handle.

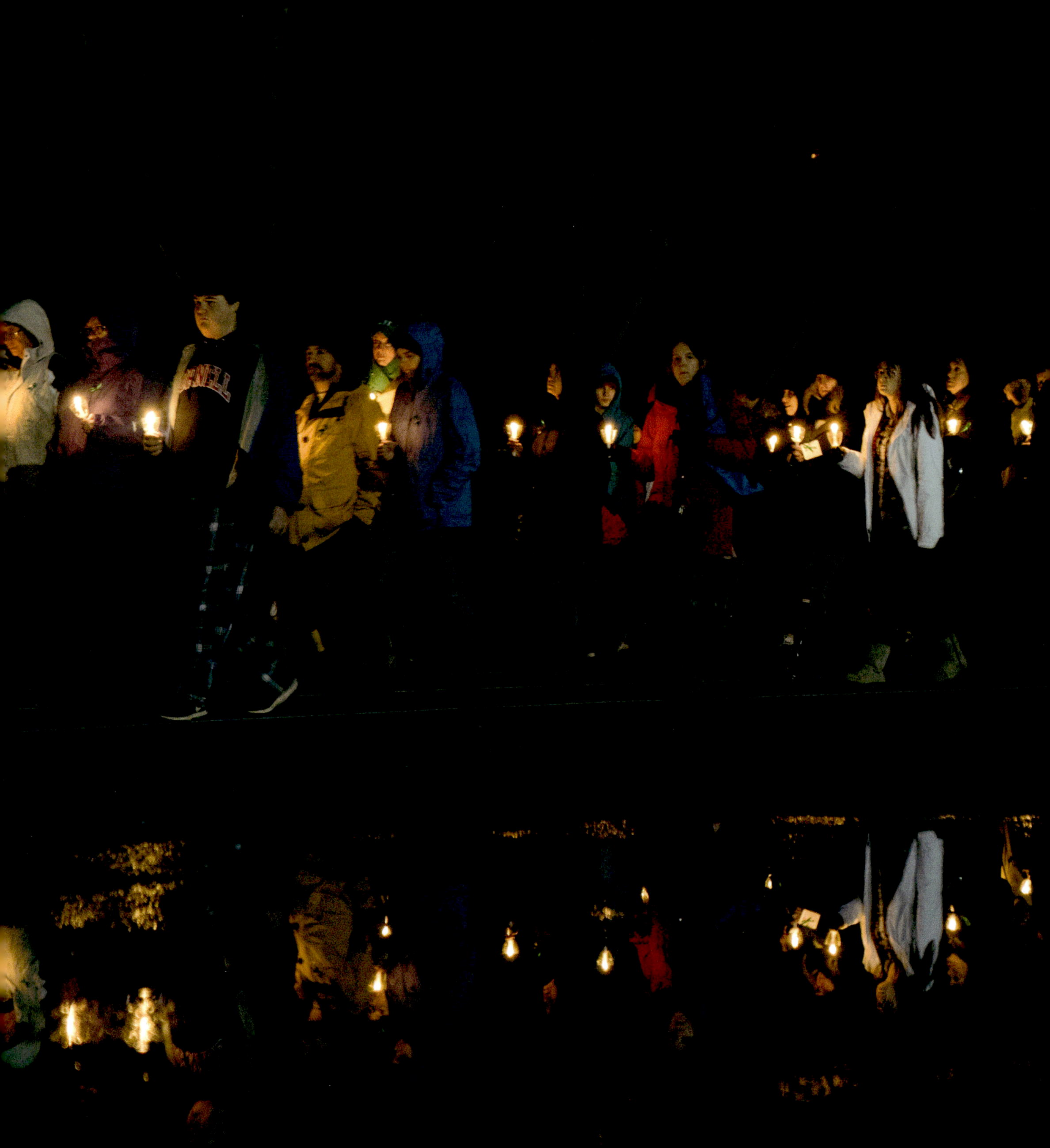

CHAPTER 3:

The Root Cause

Why does someone commit a mass shooting? What causes them to inflict harm on other people? One theory involves mental health, that the person behind a mass shooting is mentally ill. Such was the case with the Sandy Hook Elementary shooter.

However, according to the National Alliance on Mental Illness, 40 percent of mass shooters did *not* show signs of illness or distress prior to their crimes. Nor did they receive a diagnosis of mental illness.

Another theory about mass shooters is that the shooter came from a broken home. Such could be the case with the Marjory Stoneman Douglas High School shooter. According to his sister, the shooter's birth mom was a prostitute who drank and did drugs while pregnant with him. After he was born, he was put up for adoption. His father died of a heart attack in front of him when he was five years old. His mother died in November 2017. He was living with family friends at the time he killed his former classmates in 2018.

A candlelight vigil honors the lives of those killed in the 2018 Marjory Stoneman Douglas High School shooting.

But countless individuals come from broken homes, and they do not commit mass shootings. In fact, the family situation was the opposite for the two Columbine High School shooters. Both boys grew up in upper middle-class families with two parents in the home. They were both involved in Boy Scouts and had jobs.

Another theory, especially when referencing young shooters, is that they were bullied or experienced childhood trauma. In 2019, about 22 percent of children ages 12 to 18 reported being bulled at school, according to the National Center for Education Statistics. Most students reported being the subject of rumors and being called names. Five percent reported physical aggression. Four percent reported being threatened with harm. According to The Violence Project's database, approximately 65 percent of school shooters experienced serious childhood trauma. Examples of trauma include physical or sexual abuse, domestic violence, or stress caused by a medical procedure or loss of a parent.

Researchers with the U.S. Secret Service and the U.S. Department of Education stated in a 2004 report that "there is no set of traits that described all—or even most—of the attackers. Instead, they varied considerably in demographic, background, and other characteristics." Further, "[t]he attackers came from a variety of family situations, ranging from intact families with numerous ties

Feelings of isolation, helplessness, and fear can lead some people to commit violent acts.

> **ZOOM IN: DEFINE "MILITIA"**
>
> The Second Amendment of the U.S. Constitution states: "A well-regulated Militia, being necessary to the security of a free State, the right of the people to keep and bear Arms, shall not be infringed." The Constitution was written in 1787 and approved, or ratified, in 1788. This amendment is hotly debated when it comes to gun rights because of how it's interpreted. People have different ideas about what a "well-regulated Militia" means.

to the community, to foster homes with histories of neglect." Note that "[m]any attackers felt bullied, persecuted, or injured by others prior to the attack."

Older shooters may be pushed to commit their crimes by rejection from a significant other, losing a job, or losing a large sum of money. That's what happened to a man in Atlanta, Georgia, on July 29, 1999. He lost more than $100,000 in two months at his job. Overwhelmed, he then shot his two children and wife (he may have killed his first wife and mother-in-law in 1993, too) before shooting people at two businesses. He wounded 13 people and killed 6 more before turning the gun on himself.

Violent video games are often blamed for mass shootings. However, there are facts to disprove this theory. First, violent video games are played around the world, and the mass shooting data does not match up. Between 1998 and 2019, the United States had 73 percent of all mass shootings in developed countries. Eighteen of those developed countries had no mass shootings at all. Second, in the United

States, more than 150 million people play video games regularly. While the three top-selling games are first-person shooting or action-adventure games, those 150 million people are not committing mass shootings. (To note: The favorite video games of the Sandy Hook shooter were *Dance Dance Revolution* and *Mario Brothers*.) Lastly, researchers at the University of New South Wales in Sydney, Australia, go so far as to say that people play violent video games "to become better as individuals" and "to overcome our fears." These kinds of games help people gain a sense of control, connect with others, and feel competent. They also allow people to express emotions, especially anger, in a safe setting.

While there are many different theories about why a person commits mass murder, discussions about mass shootings always include one common word: *guns*. Some people believe in eliminating all guns to solve the problem. Others believe in arming everyone. And then there are most U.S. citizens who believe in something in between.

In the United States, there are an estimated 120 guns per 100 citizens. That is more than twice the number of guns per 100 people in the country of Yemen, in the Middle East, and three times the number of guns in Serbia, in Eastern Europe. A Swiss research project estimated that there were 390 million guns in the United States in 2018. Every time a mass shooting happens, gun-control activists call on Congress to pass laws to make it harder to get guns.

From 1994 to 2004, a law ended the sale or manufacture of 14 kinds of semiautomatic assault weapons. Data shows that before the ban, mass shooting deaths involving assault rifles were rising.

But during the ban, the number of deaths slowed. In addition, the number of deaths from mass shootings in general fell. When the assault rifle ban ended in 2004, there was an almost immediate rise in mass shooting deaths. While the ban was likely responsible for the drop in mass shootings, it did not appear to substantially curb gun violence in general. Some researchers suggested a longer ban could've made more of a difference. Ten states still have laws with various bans and restrictions on assault weapons.

Nineteen states and the District of Columbia have a "red-flag law" in place. It allows law enforcement to remove a firearm from a person who is believed to be at high risk of committing a crime before an actual crime is committed. From 2016 to 2023, California's red-flag law prevented 58 potential mass shootings and other instances of gun violence.

In 2022, Congress passed the Bipartisan Safer Communities Act. This bill ensured that gun buyers under 21 years old got background checks. It provided mental health services. The bill also prevented convicted domestic abusers from buying a gun for five years—the "boyfriend loophole." In addition, the bill helped define what a gun seller is and outlined penalties for gun trafficking.

After a mass shooting, gun rights groups make their own arguments regarding restrictive gun laws. "It's the not the guns, it's the people" is a common statement. They stress gun training and education. They say society needs "good guys with guns." This

36 — EXAMINING MASS SHOOTINGS

Lawmakers spend countless hours debating how to best keep gun violence from escalating.

ZOOM IN: UNITED STATES FIRST IN GUN DEATHS

Rates of firearm homicides among high-income countries with populations over 10 million

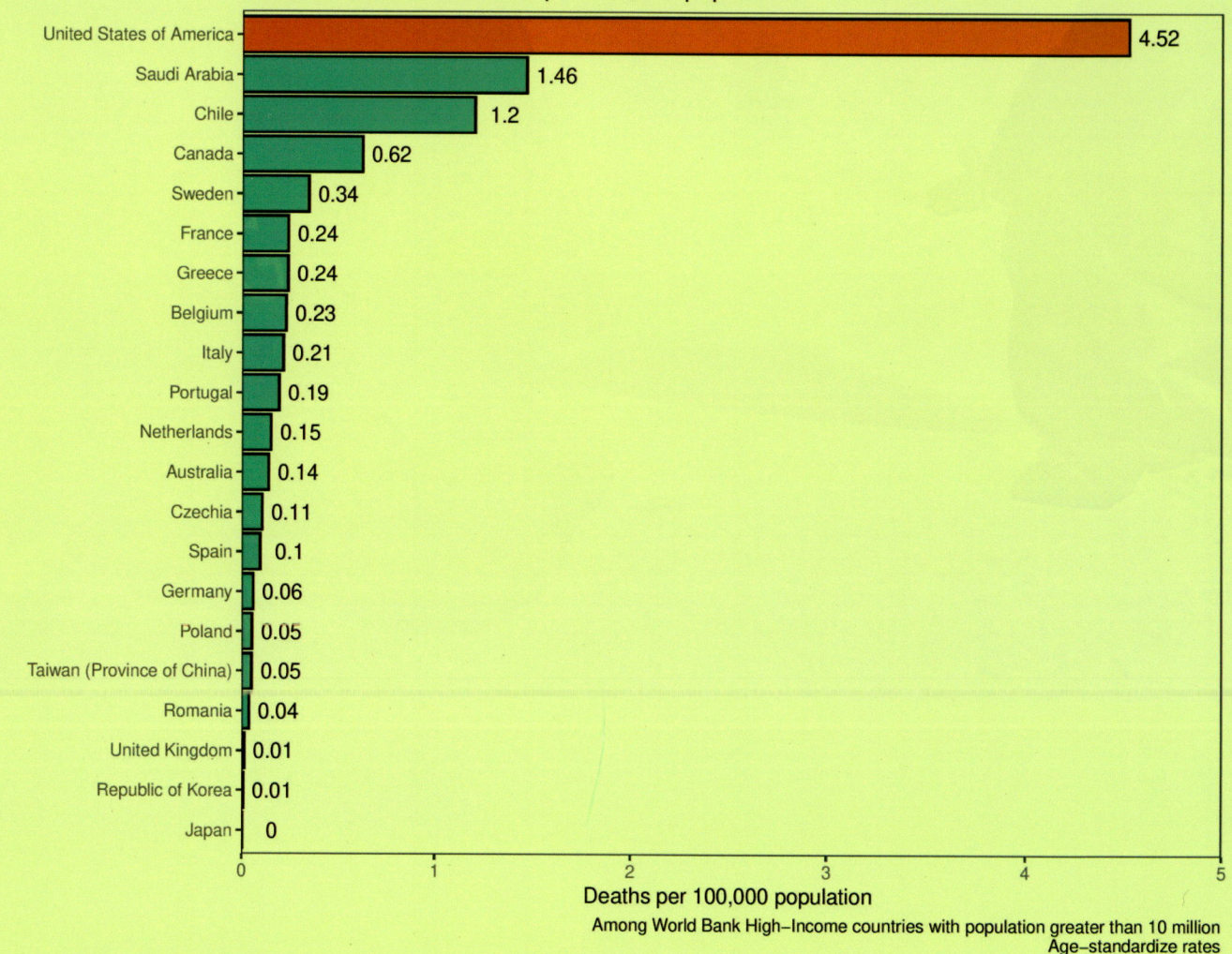

Rates of firearm homicides per 100,000 population

United States of America	4.52
Saudi Arabia	1.46
Chile	1.2
Canada	0.62
Sweden	0.34
France	0.24
Greece	0.24
Belgium	0.23
Italy	0.21
Portugal	0.19
Netherlands	0.15
Australia	0.14
Czechia	0.11
Spain	0.1
Germany	0.06
Poland	0.05
Taiwan (Province of China)	0.05
Romania	0.04
United Kingdom	0.01
Republic of Korea	0.01
Japan	0

Deaths per 100,000 population
Among World Bank High-Income countries with population greater than 10 million
Age-standardize rates

Source: Scott Glenn, IHME

involves putting more guns in the hands of trained, responsible gun owners in schools and public spaces. Doing so, they say, would keep people safe from "bad guys." It would allow for quicker response times when a shooting occurs, saving more lives.

However, according to the FBI, "good guys with guns" interrupted mass shootings only 4 percent of the time between 2000 and 2018. Unarmed civilians interrupted shootings almost 12 percent of the time—three times more often. In nearly 7 percent of the cases, it's the shooters themselves who end the horror by committing suicide.

A large concern for gun owners is that their guns will be taken away if gun-control activists prevail. They claim their Second Amendment rights will be denied if lawmakers regulate guns or ban assault weapons nationwide. Some gun-control activists accuse gun owners of being more concerned about their weapons than people's lives. A lobbyist at the 2018 National Rifle Association annual meeting addressed that belief: "You don't have a monopoly on caring," he said. "You don't have a monopoly on grieving, and you certainly don't have a monopoly on solutions."

CHAPTER 4:
Finding Solutions

> Marches, rallies, and school walk-outs are ways in which people can make their voices heard.

Everyone can agree that innocent people should not be dying from gun violence. But how can we, as a society, prevent future mass shootings?

Focusing on gun control may be one solution, since data does show that stronger gun laws help prevent deaths. There would be several pieces to this:

- Ban the sale of assault weapons.
- Limit access to assault weapons and high-capacity magazines, which hold more than the usual rounds of ammunition.
- Have background checks on all gun sales and close loopholes at gun shows.
- Put Extreme Risk Laws into place that restrict access to guns if there are warning signs that a person may try to hurt others.

In addition:

- Create safe storage campaigns.
- Raise the minimum age to purchase a gun.
- Require waiting periods.
- Have a single national gun database.
- Track gun-related deaths nationwide.

STOP
GUN
IOLENCE
BAN ASSAULT
STYLE RIFLES!
BAN OVERSIZE
WORTH
FIRE

- Track all shootings by gun type, ammunition, if the gun was legally possessed, if the shooter was permitted to carry a concealed firearm, and if the shooter was a felon.

Another solution for preventing mass shootings may be to focus on violence prevention programs. These programs strengthen communities and neighborhoods. Some programs have outreach providers who help when there are conflicts. Hospitals have similar programs that provide support and services to gun violence survivors. The idea is that the more neighbors know about and care for each other, the safer they will be.

Better mental health services can play a huge role in curbing gun violence. Studies by the FBI and the U.S. Secret Service found that not only were shooters depressed, but they were also feeling desperate. Perhaps attackers had been struggling for some time and not getting help. Their struggles turned to humiliation and anger. They could have felt isolated and alone. Experts believe that supporting someone in crisis can prevent a tragedy. Letting those in crisis know they can receive help without fear of expulsion or jail time can save lives. Proactive responses are more beneficial than reactive responses.

Unfortunately, the entire country is in a crisis of its own. The mental health field is understaffed. Most states have fewer than 40 percent of the providers they need. After the Sandy Hook Elementary shooting, Nicole Hockley started Sandy Hook Promise. Her six-year-old son Dylan had been killed that fateful day. Sandy Hook Promise trains people on how to identify others who might be in crisis and how to help them.

ZOOM IN: NO NAMES

An organization called No Notoriety was started in Aurora, Colorado, by Tom and Caren Teves after their 24-year-old son was killed at the movie theater mass shooting. They were shocked that the shooter got so much media attention, while the victims did not. Killers want this kind of attention for their acts. And, horribly, it means the next killers are watching. The No Notoriety Protocol means there is minimal coverage of the shooter. Even some news stations won't announce the shooter's name and will focus only on the victims and their stories, as well as the first responders.

Texas, the state that had nine mass shootings between 2009 and 2023, including the tragedy at Robb Elementary, has one of the lowest mental health spending rates in the nation. According to Mental Health America, access in Texas to special education, insurance, treatment, cost of insurance, and mental health workforce is ranked last.

Hand in hand with mental health is the idea of changing a hateful ideology. Researchers at Hamline University say that even though the number of hate-driven mass shootings is small, it is increasing. "I think it's really important that we tackle that hate, especially . . . when we talk about social media and where young people are getting access to this type of hate online," said Dr. Jillian Peterson, an associate professor of criminology and criminal justice at Hamline.

The number of mass shootings in the United States continues to rise, and the time between incidents continues to shrink. No type of venue is immune to the violence: offices, schools, shopping malls, places of worship, grocery stores, entertainment facilities, restaurants. Neither is any age, race, gender, or religious belief. A shooting isn't a headline anymore unless a certain number of people are killed. Tragically, mass shootings have, in a sense, become a way of life in the United States.

While there is no one solution to preventing mass shootings, people can agree that any step toward potentially saving a life is a good one. In the years ahead, groups will continue to push for gun regulations and mental health assistance. They will continue to raise awareness of the roles guns play in our lives and encourage education and safety training. With cooperation and compassion, the country's leaders and citizens can reverse the trend.

Getting Real

SUE KLEBOLD

In November 2016, Sue Klebold stood in front of an audience and told them about the last time she heard her son's voice. He was heading to Columbine High School the morning of April 20, 1999. All she heard him say was, "Bye," before he and another student went to school and murdered 13 people. For years, Klebold felt that she had failed as a mother because of what her son did. She didn't learn that he had been cutting himself and wanted to commit suicide two years before the massacre until she read about it in his notebooks months after the tragedy. She also watched videotapes of the two boys. She couldn't believe her son was the same person. She felt her son's final violent act was "rooted not in a desire to kill but in his desire to die."

Many people asked Klebold how she didn't know what her son was planning. She later learned that about half of families with children who have suicidal thoughts or behaviors don't know their children are struggling. Klebold's mission today is suicide prevention. She believes that not only can suicide be prevented, but mass violence can, too, since research shows that mass shooters are often suicidal.

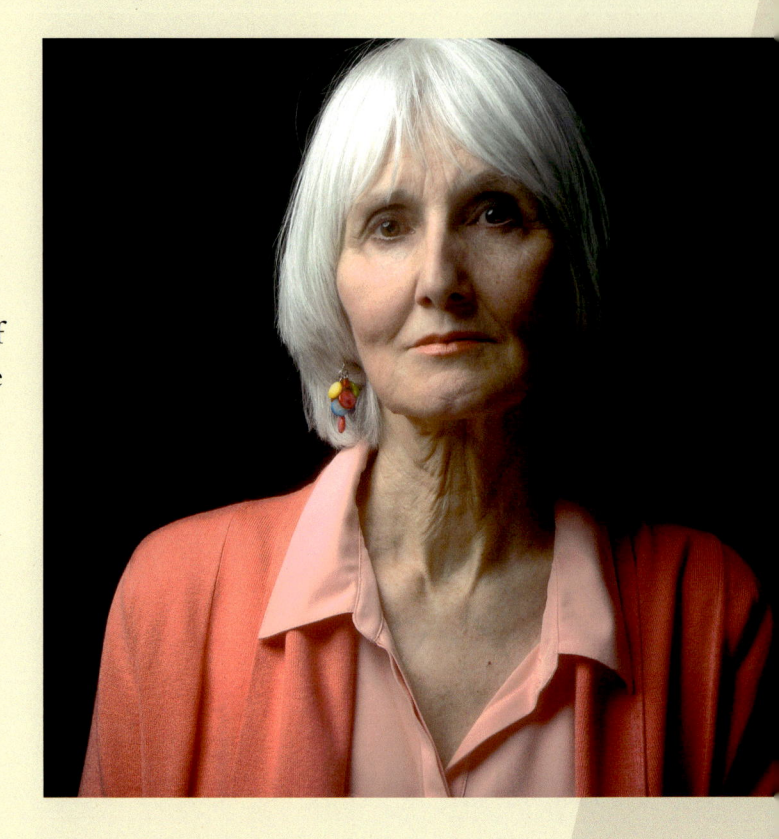

Klebold is also an advocate for mental health. Money she makes from her book, *A Mother's Reckoning: Living in the Aftermath of Tragedy*, goes to research and charitable organizations that focus on mental health.

DR. JILLIAN PETERSON AND DR. JAMES DENSLEY

Two people committed to better understanding violence and its causes are Dr. Jillian Peterson and Dr. James Densley. Peterson has spent years studying people behind violent acts, including those facing the death penalty. As an associate professor of criminology and criminal justice at Hamline University in St. Paul, Minnesota, Peterson and a team of Hamline students built a database of every mass shooter since 1966. Densley was a special education teacher in New York City public schools before earning his doctorate in sociology. He has researched criminal networks, street gangs, and violence.

Together, Peterson and Densley co-founded The Violence Prevention Project Research Center, or The Violence Project, in St. Paul. The Mass Shooter Database on The Violence Project's website has influenced policies and received a lot of national media attention.

The Violence Project is "dedicated to reducing violence through research." The nonprofit organization is known for its expertise in gun violence prevention, street gangs, violent extremism, and youth violence. But the staff has also developed mental illness crisis intervention and de-escalation training for law enforcement called The R-Model.

Peterson and Densley wrote an award-winning book called the *The Violence Project: How to Stop a Mass Shooting Epidemic*. In it, they interviewed survivors, first responders, and victims' families. They also interviewed mass shooters themselves to better understand the shooters' path to violence and how to develop strategies to prevent future tragedies.

Timeline

1949
Camden, New Jersey: 13 people killed

1966
University of Texas, Austin: 17 people killed, 30+ wounded

1984
San Ysidro, California; McDonald's: 21 people killed, 19 wounded

1991
Killeen, Texas; Luby's Cafeteria: 23 people killed, 20 wounded

1994–2004
A bill suspends the sale or manufacture of 14 kinds of semi-automatic assault weapons

1999
Littleton, Colorado; Columbine High School: 13 people killed, 24 wounded

2007
Blacksburg, Virginia; Virginia Tech: 32 people killed, 17 wounded

2009
Fort Hood, Texas: 13 people killed, 32 wounded

2012
Aurora, Colorado; Century 16 movie theater: 12 people killed, 70+ wounded

2012
Newtown, Connecticut; Sandy Hook Elementary: 27 people killed, 2 wounded

2016
Orlando, Florida; Pulse Nightclub: 49 people killed, 50+ wounded

2017
Las Vegas, Nevada; Route 91 Harvest music festival: 58 people killed, 400+ wounded

2017
Sutherland Springs, Texas; First Baptist Church: 26 people killed, 20 wounded

2018
Parkland, Florida; Marjory Stoneman Douglas High School: 17 people killed, 14 wounded

2019
El Paso, Texas; Walmart: 23 people killed, 22 wounded

2022
Buffalo, New York: Tops Friendly Markets supermarket: 10 people killed, 3 wounded

2022
Uvalde, Texas; Robb Elementary: 21 people killed, 17 wounded

2022
Congress passes the Bipartisan Safer Communities Act.

2023
Monterey Park, California; Star Dance Studio: 11 people killed, 10 wounded

2023
Nashville, Tennessee; The Covenant School: 6 people killed

Glossary

casualty—a person who is wounded or dies in an incident

confrontation—an angry face-to-face meeting

domestic—relating to a home or family

extremist—a person who holds beliefs or views that are radical

LGBTQ+—relating to people who identify as lesbian, gay, bisexual, transgender, queer, and more

livestream—to put an event on the Internet or social media while it's taking place

loophole—a way of avoiding a law

manifesto—a public statement of intent, motive, and/or beliefs

militia—a body of citizen soldiers used in emergencies

paranoid—feeling or experiencing unreasonable suspicion of others

protocol—a rule, plan, or procedure

psychiatric—relating to mental, emotional, or behavior issues

rampage—violent, angry behavior that is uncontrolled and destructive

trafficking—the practice of dealing or trading something illegally

Selected Bibliography

Follman, Mark. *Trigger Points: Inside the Mission to Stop Mass Shootings in America.* New York: Dey St., 2022.

Greenfieldboyce, Nell. "Research shows policies that may help prevent mass shootings—and some that don't." Public Health: MPR News. NPR. May 26, 2022. https://www.npr.org/sections/health-shots/2022/05/26/1101423558/how-can-mas-shootings-be-prevented-definitive-answers-are-hard-to-come-by.

Klebold, Sue. *A Mother's Reckoning: Living in the Aftermath of Tragedy.* New York: Broadway Books, 2017.

National Institute of Justice. "Public Mass Shootings: Database Amasses Details of a Half Century of U.S. Mass Shootings with Firearms, Generating Psychosocial Histories." February 3, 2022. https://nij.ojp.gov/topics/articles/public-mass-shootings-database-amasses-details-half-century-us-mass-shootings.

Peterson, Jillian, PhD, and James Densley, PhD. *The Violence Project: How to Stop a Mass Shooting Epidemic.* New York: Abrams Press, 2021.

Schweit, Katherine. *Stop the Killing: How to End the Mass Shooting Crisis.* Lanham, MD: Rowman & Littlefield, 2021.

Websites

Britannica: Mass Shooting

https://www.britannica.com/topic/mass-shooting

Explore real-time maps, charts, and graphs related to mass shootings in the United States.

Everytown for Gun Safety

https://everytownresearch.org/mass-shootings-in-america

Review mass shooting statistics and possible solutions.

Index

cause theories
   broken homes, 31–32
   childhood trauma, 32
   loss, 32
   mental health, 18, 31, 36, 42, 43, 44, 45
   violent video games, 34–35
churches. *See* houses of worship
clubs, 16–17, 46
definitions, 8
Densley, James, 45
domestic violence, 28, 29, 32, 36
extremism, 15, 16, 45
first "modern" mass shooting, 11–12, 46
gun numbers (U.S.), 35
gun rights, 8, 34, 35, 36, 39
gun sales, 8, 35, 36, 40
houses of worship, 15–16, 17, 46
Inland Regional Center (2015), 16
Klebold, Sue, 44
legislation, 8, 24, 34, 35, 36, 39, 40, 46
locations
   Aurora, Colorado (2012), 15, 42, 46
   Austin, Texas (1966), 11, 46
   Blacksburg, Virginia (2007), 12, 46
   Boulder, Colorado (2021), 18
   Buffalo, New York (2022), 18, 46
   Camden, New Jersey (1949), 8, 11, 46
   Charleston, South Carolina (2015), 15
   El Paso, Texas (2019), 17, 46
   Fort Hood, Texas (2009), 15, 46
   Killeen, Texas (1991), 12, 46
   Las Vegas, Nevada (2017), 18, 46
   Littleton, Colorado (1999), 12, 46
   Monterey Park, California (2023), 18, 46
   Nashville, Tennessee (2023), 46
   Newtown, Connecticut (2012), 22, 25, 46
   Orlando, Florida (2016), 16, 46
   Parkland, Florida (2018), 27, 46
   Pittsburgh, Pennsylvania (2018), 17
   San Bernardino, California (2015), 16, 17
   San Ysidro, California (1984), 11–12, 46
   Sutherland Springs, Texas (2017), 17, 46
   Uvalde, Texas (2022), 27, 46
Lunar New Year's Eve (2023), 18
military connections, 8, 16, 46
movie theater, 15, 28, 42, 46
music festival, 18, 46
No Notoriety, 42
Peterson, Jillian, 43, 45
racial motivation, 15–16, 17
restaurants, 11–12, 43, 46
safety protocols, 24, 25, 27, 28
schools
   Columbine High School (1999), 12, 21, 22, 24, 27, 32, 44, 46
   The Covenant School (2023), 46
   Jackson State University (1970), 24
   Jonesboro, Arkansas (1998), 24
   Kent State (1970), 22
   Marjory Stoneman Douglas High School (2018), 27, 31, 46
   Robb Elementary (2022), 27, 43, 46
   Sandy Hook Elementary (2012), 22, 25, 27, 31, 35, 42, 46
   University of Texas (1966), 10, 11, 46
   Virginia Tech (2007), 12, 15, 46
semiautomatic weapons, 2, 12, 15, 16, 17, 35, 46
shooter names, 42
social media, 17, 18, 22, 43
solutions, 39, 40, 42, 43
stores, 17, 18, 43, 46
worst mass shooting, 18, 46